LEVEL **1** For first r

* short, straightforward sentences
* basic, fun vocabulary
* simple, easy-to-follow stories of up to 100 words
* large print and easy-to-read design

LEVEL **2** For developing readers

* longer sentences
* simple vocabulary, introducing new words
* longer stories of up to 200 words
* bold design, to capture readers' interest

LEVEL **3** For more confident readers

* longer sentences with varied structure
* wider vocabulary
* high-interest stories of up to 300 words
* smaller print for experienced readers

LEVEL **4** For able readers

* longer sentences with complex structure
* rich, exciting vocabulary
* complex stories of up to 400 words
* emphasis on text more than illustrations

3

Make Reading Fun!

Once you have read the story, you will find some amazing activities at the back of the book! There are Excellent Exercises for you to complete, plus a super Picture Dictionary.

But first it is time for the story . . .

Ready?

Steady?

Let's read!

Ready Steady Read!

Dear Parents,

Congratulations! Your child has embarked on an exciting journey – they're learning to read! As a parent, you can be there to support and cheer them along as they take their first steps.

At school, children are taught how to decode words and arrange these building blocks of language into sentences and wonderful stories.

At home, parents play a vital part in reinforcing these new-found skills. You can help your child practise their reading by providing well-written, engaging stories, which you can enjoy together.

This series – **Ready, Steady, Read!** – offers exactly that, and more. These stories support inexperienced readers by:

- gradually introducing new vocabulary
- using repetition to consolidate learning
- gradually increasing sentence length and word count
- providing texts that boost a young reader's confidence.

As each book is completed, engaging activities encourage young readers to look back at the story, while a Picture Dictionary reinforces new vocabulary. Enjoyment is the key – and reading together can be great fun for both parent and child!

Prue Goodwin
Lecturer in Literacy and Children's Books

C015628896

How to use this series

The **Ready, Steady, Read!** series has 4 levels. The facing page shows what you can expect to find in the books at each level.

As your child's confidence grows, they can progress to books from the higher levels. These will keep them engaged and encourage new reading skills.

The levels are only meant as guides; together, you and your child can pick the book that will be just right.

Here are some handy tips for helping children who are ready for reading!

Give them choice – Letting children pick a book (from the level that's right for them) makes them feel involved.

Talk about it – Discussing the story and the pictures helps children engage with the book.

Read it again – Repetition of favourite stories reinforces learning.

Cheer them on! – Praise and encouragement builds a child's confidence and the belief in their growing ability.

Michael Coleman   Gwyneth Williamson

Ridiculous!

LITTLE TIGER PRESS
London

"Winter is here," yawned Mr Tortoise.

"Time for bed," yawned Mrs Tortoise.

"But I don't want to go to bed," said Shelley. "I want to see what winter is like."

"*Ridiculous!*" cried Mr and
Mrs Tortoise.
"Whoever heard of a tortoise
outside in winter?"

Soon Mr and Mrs Tortoise
were snoring . . .

But Shelley went outside.

Soon a duck spotted her. "A tortoise out in winter?" he quacked.

"*Ridiculous!* You don't have a beak.
How will you break through the ice?"
Shelley shrugged. "He's right," she
thought. "I can't do that."

Then she met a dog. "A tortoise out
in winter?" he barked.

"*Ridiculous!* You can't run around
like me. How will you keep warm?"
Shelley didn't know.

Then she saw a cat.

"A tortoise out in winter?" she
miaowed. "*Ridiculous!* You're too
slow. How will you get out of
the cold?"

Shelley wasn't sure.

Shelley trudged up a hill, where
she met a bird.

"A tortoise out in winter?"
she cheeped. "*Ridiculous!*
How will you fly home to
your family?"

Shelley gulped. "I can't fly,"
she thought. "I can't even hop!"

A tear trickled down her cheek.
"They're right," she thought.
"A tortoise out in winter *is*
ridiculous."

Suddenly she slipped on
some ice . . .

and began to slide down the hill,
faster and faster . . .

. . . faster
than the
dog . . .

faster than
the *cat* . . .

until she hit
a bump and
flew through
the air like
a *bird*!

She landed on the pond and
slithered towards her shed.

But it was covered with ice.

"How will you break through?"
laughed the duck.

"With my shell!" cried Shelley.
And she smashed her way through
the ice, and into her home!

"You haven't been outside, have you, Shelley?" asked Mrs Tortoise, sleepily. "Outside?" said Shelley. "Whoever heard of a tortoise out in winter?"

"Ridiculous!"

Have you read the story? Well done! Now it is time for more fun!

Here are some questions about the story. Ask an adult to listen to your answers, and help if you get stuck.

Wonderful Winter

This story is about Shelley's winter adventure. Can you think of all the things that *you* like to do in winter?

Bits and Bobs

Can you name some of the objects in this shed? Do you have any of these things at *your* house?

Playful Puppy

Now describe what Dog is doing in this picture.

Warm and Cosy

Can you remember how Shelley broke through the ice into her home? How do *you* normally get into your house?

Picture Dictionary

Can you read all of these words from the story?

bird

cat

dog

duck

hill

shell

slide

smashed

snoring

tortoise

Can you think of any other words that describe these pictures – for example, what colours can you see? Why not try to spell some of these words? Ask an adult to help!

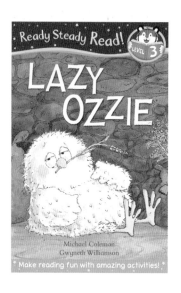

Lazy Ozzie

Lazy Ozzie is too lazy to learn how to fly. So he thinks of a brilliant plan to fool his mum into thinking he can. But will Ozzie's mum be so easily fooled . . . ?

Little Mouse and the Big Red Apple

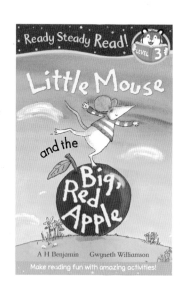

Mouse does not want to share his big, juicy apple but he is too small to move it on his own. Can he get his friends to help and still eat it all himself?